Modern Curriculum Press
BEGINNING TO READ Series

The Little Runaway

THE LITTLE RUNAWAY

ISBN 0-8136-5552-8 Hardbound

ISBN 0-8136-5052-6 Paperback

14 15 16 17 18 19 20 99 98 97 96 95

The Little Runaway

Margaret Hillert

Illustrated by Irv Anderson

MODERN CURRICULUM PRESS
Cleveland • Toronto

Here is a mother.

Here is a little baby.

Come here, little one.

Come here to me.

No, no.

I want to go away.

Here I go.

One, two, three.

Away, away.

It is fun to run away.

Away I go.

I can run.

I can jump.

I can play.

Look up, look up.

Something is up.

Something can go away.

See it go away.

Away, away, away.

I see something.

Something red.

Something yellow.

Down, down, down.

See something come down.

It is fun to play here.

Look up, up, up.

See the little balls.

Little and red.

Oh, oh, oh.

Oh, my.

Oh, my.

It is not funny.

Here is something blue.

I can look down in it.

Help, help!

Oh, oh.

I want to go away.

Work, work, work.

You can work.

I see you work.

Come and play.

We can play.

Up, up, up.

I can not go up.

Oh my, oh my.

Something big.

Big, big, big.

Oh, oh, oh.

Where is my mother?

Help, help.

Mother, Mother, I want you.

I want my mother.

It is not fun to run away.

Here, little one.

Here is Mother.

Come to Mother.

Margaret Hillert, author of several books in the MCP Beginning-To-Read Series, is a writer, poet, and teacher.

The Little Runaway

The story of a runaway kitten, with charming illustrations and a text that uses only 45 preprimer words.

Word List

7 here
is
a
mother
little
baby
8 come
one
to
me
9 no
I
want
go
away
two
three
10 it
fun
run
11 can
jump
play
12 look
up
something
13 see
14 red
yellow
15 down
16 the
balls
17 oh
my
not
funny
18 blue
in
19 help
21 work
you
22 and
we
24 big
25 where